No Peanuts for Pete

No Peanuts for Pete

Archway Publishing books may be ordered through booksellers or by contacting:

Archway Publishing
1663 Liberty Drive
Bloomington, IN 47403
www.archwaypublishing.com
1 (888) 242-5904

ISBN: 978-1-4808-3651-8 (sc)
ISBN: 978-1-4808-3653-2 (hc)
ISBN: 978-1-4808-3652-5 (e)

Print information available on the last page.

First Printing, 2016

Archway Publishing rev. date: 9/7/2016

Peanuts for Pete

Written by
Christina Roderick

Illustrated by
Anne Zimanski

To Emma,
Dream Big!
Your Friend,

Christina
Roderick

For Nolan and Landon,

Life's greatest gift is the privilege of being your mother.

You both inspire me everyday.

Halloween was coming and Pete was excited. It was his favorite holiday. He raced out of bed on Saturday morning and begged his mom to take him shopping for his costume.

"Not today," Mom replied. "We have to go to soccer, then swimming, and then to Lucas's birthday party. Maybe tomorrow, honey."

The next day was Sunday. Pete woke up while it was still dark outside and snuck into his parents' bedroom.

"Psst…Mom? Are you awake? Can we go shopping for my costume today?"

"Yes, Pete," Mom replied with a sigh. "But it's four in the morning! Go back to bed."

Pete did as he was told, but he was too excited to sleep. What kind of costume will I choose? he wondered. Maybe I will be a super hero…
or a vampire. Yes, a vampire, now that is scary. Or maybe I will dress up as a fireman. There are too many choices! Pete thought, feeling worn out from thinking about all his options. How will I ever choose?

After breakfast, Pete dressed, and Mom said they could go to the store to buy his costume. But when they went outside, they saw that Mom's car had a flat tire.

"Sorry, Pete," she said. "We can't go to the store until my tire is fixed."

By the time they fixed the tire, it was dark outside again, and the store was closed. Pete worried that he would never get to the costume store.

On Monday, Mom picked Pete up from school and took him straight to the costume shop. But when they got there, they couldn't find any of the costumes Pete wanted. All that were left were princesses and witches. Pete started to cry.

"Don't worry," Mom said. "We will find a way to fix this. I promise."

On Tuesday, Mom and Pete looked at pictures of costumes until he found the perfect one. That night, she went to the fabric store and bought supplies.
They might not have been able to find the costume Pete wanted in stores, but that wouldn't stop Mom from *making* him the best costume ever!

The next weekend was Halloween. Pete was invited to a Halloween party at Libby Rogers's house. He watched the clock all day until it was finally 5:00 p.m.—time to get dressed for the party.

Pete ran upstairs to find his costume. He carefully got dressed into his pirate costume, placing the hat on his head, the patch over his eye and the sword sheath on his belt to complete the outfit. Admiring himself in the mirror, Pete let out an "arrr" and bounded down the stairs to find his friend Lucas waiting for him, dressed as a ninja.

"Wow! Cool costume, Pete," Lucas said. "Are you ready to go to Libby's party?"

"Yup! Let's go," Pete replied, and they headed for the door.

"Wait just a second, boys!" Mom called, sounding concerned. "Pete, where is your epi-shot?"

"It's right here, Mom," Pete responded as he pulled the medicine stick out of his sword's sheath.

"Very clever, Pete," she said. "Be careful." With that, Mom watched Lucas and Pete run across the street to Libby's party.

When they arrived, all of the kids from the neighborhood were there. Cobwebs covered the walls and ceiling in Libby's basement. Spooky music was playing, and there was even a fog machine! Everyone was having a good time.

Everyone, that is, except Pete. He took one look at all of the party food then locked himself in the laundry room.

Knock, knock.

"Pete, it's Libby. Open up! What's wrong?"

"I can't stay at your party, Libby," Pete explained. "I need to call my mom and go home right away."

A few minutes later, there was another knock on the door.

"Who is it?" Pete asked.

"It's Mrs. Rogers. Could you please open the door a crack and talk to me?" she asked.

Pete cracked the door just enough to see Mrs. Rogers with one eye.

"Now, sweetheart," she began, "what happened? Are you sick? Are you hurt? Libby tells me that you want to leave the party, but you just got here!"

"No, Mrs. Rogers, I am not sick or hurt. I don't want to leave the party," Pete explained. "I have to leave the party. I have to leave because there are peanuts everywhere! Wherever I look, there are chocolate peanut butter eyeballs and peanut butter crunchy bars, and even the cheesy doodle snack mix has peanuts in it! I am allergic to peanuts, Mrs. Rogers. It's not safe for me to stay. Thank you for having me." Pete slammed the laundry room door again.

Knock, knock, knock.

"Pete," Mrs. Rogers said, "it might be hard for you to go home if you won't come out of the laundry room. Can you come out for just a minute?"

Reluctantly, Pete came out of the laundry room and sadly looked up at Mrs. Rogers.

"Now, Pete," she said with a soft voice, "you are Libby's friend, and we all want you to stay at this party and be safe. So how about if I take away all of the peanut snacks and find some that are safe for you and that everyone can enjoy? Then would you stay?"

"Well, ummm, I think I can stay," Pete responded, "except for one more problem—do you think all of the kids could wash their hands, just in case they have any peanut butter on them?"

"I am sure we can arrange that," she said with a smile.

A few minutes later, the party was transformed. All of the party guests had freshly washed hands and peanut-free snacks.

Pete played hide-and-seek and ate potato chips until his belly felt as if it was going to explode!

Then everyone watched a scary movie – but not too scary - until it was time to go home.

When Pete's mom arrived to pick him up, Pete noticed that Mrs. Rogers gave Mom a little wink before she waved goodbye. Mom just smiled and asked Pete if he had a good time at the party.

"Sure, Mom," he told her. "It was the best party ever!"

"Oh good, I'm glad you had fun. Were there any peanut-free snacks for you to eat?" she asked.

"Well…" Pete said, with hesitation in his voice. "Hmmm…yes. Yes, all of the snacks were peanut-free."

"That's a relief!" Mom exclaimed with a little smirk as they walked home.

Pete didn't tell Mom about what had happened at the party. He didn't want her to worry, but somehow, he thought, she might already know.

Christina Roderick is a mom inspired by her six-year-old son with a mission to educate others about the dangers of food allergies. She has had a successful career in medical sales and volunteers for a nonprofit pediatric cancer organization. She lives with her husband, Shayne, and her two boys, Nolan and Landon, in the Boston area.

Photo credit: Mike Scott

CPSIA information can be obtained
at www.ICGtesting.com
Printed in the USA
BVOW07s1952190916
462651BV00003B/3/P